Shannon

The Schoolmarm Mysteries
San Francisco, 1880

by Kathleen V. Kudlinski

illustrated by
Bill Farnsworth

GIRLHOOD JOURNEYS™ COLLECTION
ALADDIN PAPERBACKS

For the real Alva and Fred Beal,
a caring nurse and a gifted teacher,
role models in excellence.

Grateful acknowledgment is made to the San Francisco History Center, San Francisco Public Library, for the illustrations on page 68 and 71; and to Corbis-Bettmann for the illustration on page 70.

First Aladdin Paperbacks edition December 1997

Aladdin Paperbacks
An imprint of Simon & Schuster
Children's Publishing Division
1230 Avenue of the Americas
New York, NY 10020

Designed by Wendy Letven Design
The text of this book is set in Garamond.

Printed and bound in Hong Kong
10 9 8 7 6 5 4 3 2 1

Library of Congress Cataloging-in-Publication Data
Kudlinski, Kathleen V.
Shannon : the schoolmarm mysteries / by Kathleen V. Kudlinski ; illustrated by Bill Farnsworth. — 1st Aladdin Paperbacks ed.
p. cm. — (Girlhood journeys)
"Girlhood journeys collection."
Summary: A recent immigrant from Ireland to San Francisco in 1880, Shannon is ready to start school, but is dismayed that her Chinese friend is forbidden by law to attend and that many of her classmates are prejudiced against the Irish as well.
ISBN 0-689-81561-1 (pbk.)
[1. Prejudices—Fiction. 2. Emigration and immigration—Fiction. 3. Irish—United States—Fiction. 4. Schools—Fiction. 5. Chinese—United States—Fiction. 6. San Francisco (Calif.)—Fiction.]
I. Farnsworth, Bill, ill. II. Title. III. Series.
PZ7.K9484St 1997
[Fic]—DC21 97-11121
CIP
AC

Contents

Chapter 1	Be Strong	5
Chapter 2	Make Your Manners	15
Chapter 3	A Wild Idea	22
Chapter 4	A Kindness	31
Chapter 5	Hot Water	37
Chapter 6	Twin Mysteries	44
Chapter 7	The Third Mystery	50
Chapter 8	Cocklebur Friends	56
Chapter 9	Sour Pickles	65
Afterword	Journey to 1880	68

CHAPTER ONE

BE STRONG

"Ouch!" Shannon squirmed. "No, dunna' stop, Mamma. It has to be perfect this morning."

"Oh, and is someone just a wee bit nervous?" Mrs. O'Brien teased. "You've gone to school before, lassie." She tried again to straighten the hair bow and smooth Shannon's wild red curls. "You've had four good years of schooling, unless I've lost count."

"But never in America, Mamma. It's sure to be different from back in Ireland."

"It's still girls and boys, a teacher and books. And what could be so strange?"

"I don't know, Mamma." Shannon tried not to bite her lip nervously. "I don't know." She looked at the new lunch pail waiting alone on the parlor table. "I wish Mi Ling could go with me."

"Now, daughter, you know the school won't allow Chinese children."

"It's not fair!" Shannon cried.

"Not fair for me, too!" Shannon's younger brother Michael stomped into the parlor followed by Mi Ling. He stuck his hands in the pockets of his knickers and kicked at a toy milk wagon on the floor.

"Michael, you're too wee a laddie to be going to school." Mamma put an arm around him. "Next year you can go with Shannon."

Michael stood taller. "Next year Mi Ling goes, too?" he asked. The Chinese girl handed him the toy and sighed.

"No," she said. "Not here in San Francisco."

"But where will you learn, Mi Ling?" Shannon asked her friend. "You're twice as smart as me." She caught her breath. "Please, please come with me!"

"Shannon, I can't," Mi Ling said quietly. "Your papa was a Good Samaritan to take me in when I needed a home, but things are harder here for the Chinese than you know."

"Nonsense! I'll get you into school somehow," Shannon promised.

Mi Ling sighed and took Michael's hand. "Come, let's play with Nanny in the nursery this morning." She looked back as they left the room. "Be strong today, Shannon."

Shannon bit her lip.

"Some things ye can change, my lassie, and some things ye canna'," Mamma said. "The trick is in knowing the difference. Now hold still." She tried again to tame Shannon's hair. "Ah, there's such fire in ye this morning! Now, go help your papa until Betsy comes to walk to school with you. He's waiting in his office."

Betsy. Shannon smiled at the thought of her lively blonde neighbor. *At least I have one friend at the new school. Only one friend, but a good one.*

"Papa, is there help you're needing?" Shannon paused at the door.

Dr. O'Brien looked up from his desk. "Ah, yes, and

there is. Pin on an apron to cover that pretty frock and wash up for me, there's a good lass." Shannon put on the pinafore and mixed a bowl of strong soap. She loved the sharp soap smell and the cold sparkle of Papa's instruments as she set them into the bath.

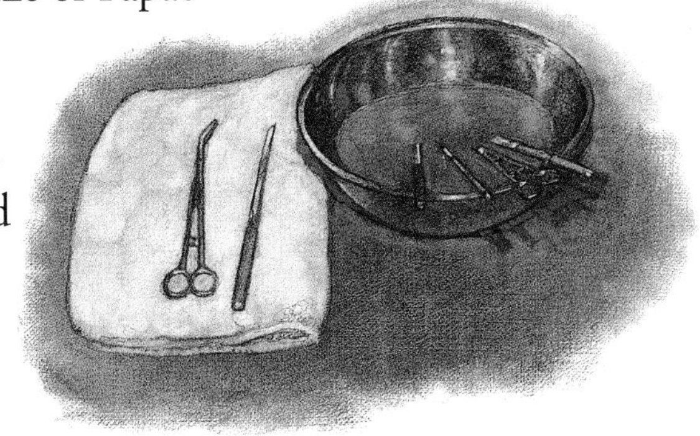

"You didn't used to wash these so often, did you, Papa?" She carefully wiped a scalpel with a sponge, laid it on a clean towel, and looked closely at it. *Was that a spot of dried blood?* Shannon shuddered and quickly dropped it back into the wash water.

"Well, Shannon, m'darlin', they're saying now that the keeping clean is very important. A newfangled idea it is: clean hands, clean table, clean wounds, clean bandages . . ."

" . . . clean forceps." Shannon set a shiny pair of tweezers on the towel, swallowed hard, and reached back into the water for the scalpel. "Does all the washing really matter?"

"Seems to keep infection down." Papa stroked his mustache. "They didn't teach it back when I went to medical school."

"Did they let Chinese people go to the medical school in Edinburgh?" Shannon asked.

"Ah, Shannon. I don't think there were many Chinese folk in Scotland or Ireland when I went to school. Are ye troubled about Mi Ling?"

"I'm troubled about everything," Shannon admitted. "New friends. A new school. A new country." She dried her hands on the apron.

"Aye, new beginnings are hard. I didn't feel any too good sailing off for America alone a year ago."

Papa worried, too? Shannon was surprised.

"As I came to know the tricks of this town and got busy with my doctoring," Dr. O'Brien went on, "it came easier." He put an arm around her shoulders. "When your mother brought you and the boys over, well, then I had all I needed." Shannon gave him a big hug.

"Thank ye for the help this morning, lassie. You've a good mind and a feel for this."

"Except—"

"I know," said Papa. "You can't stand the sight of blood."

A knock sounded from the door of his office.

"Shannon?" Betsy called. "We've got to skedaddle!"

"Coming, Betsy!" Shannon cried. She gave Papa another hug and ran to join her neighbor.

"I can't wait for you to meet my friends!" Betsy gushed. "They'll welcome you like a desert welcomes rain. There's Jeanette and Margaret, and Rebecca, of course. You've met her. And there's so many more."

Shannon followed her friend out to the porch and down onto the street. *Other friends?* she thought. *Many others?* Worries flooded her mind again. What were Betsy's friends like? Would Betsy still be her best friend with all these old friends around? What if they didn't like her?

"Look lively!" Betsy said as Shannon bumped right into her. Before them, the street corner was crowded with carriages. "Now!" Betsy cried. Grabbing Shannon's hand, she hurried across the street, weaving around a milk wagon, a

buggy, and a carriage. They jumped over a pile of horse droppings and threaded their way behind a fancy coach.

"Look out!" a farmer yelled, hauling back on his horse's reins. The palomino gagged and stopped, and the farmer shook his head.

"Sorry, sir!" Shannon called, though she was sorrier for the horse than its rider. The girls hurried on.

Traffic was even worse on Bayview Street. Horses neighed and shook their harnesses. Their hooves clattered uneasily on the steep hill. Soon, traffic came to a halt. "Whoa there!" drivers cried, and, "Steady there." Passengers stuck their heads out of closed coaches or stood tall on wagon seats, calling, "Move them out!" and "Clear the way!" Betsy and Shannon kept walking.

Halfway up the hill, they came to a wagon blocking the road. "Come on, Flossie," the wagon driver pleaded with a swaybacked bay who was leaning sideways in her traces. "Give it a try for old Zeke." He grabbed the harness and tried to help the mare pull the wagon out of the way. The horse's sides were heaving with effort, but the wagon wasn't going anywhere.

"Use yore whip!" an angry voice called.

"Poor, poor old thing," Shannon said, stopping.

"I've seen worse," Betsy said. "Back at the railroad camp they'd work a horse till it dropped. 'Course, they did the same with the Chinese workers." Shannon caught her breath. "Oh, look," Betsy went on, "there's Margaret and Jeanette!" She pulled Shannon along with one hand. With the other, she waved wildly. "Slow your paces!" she yelled to the girls.

"Oh, Betsy, my dear!" The taller girl hugged Betsy and

kissed both of her cheeks. "It's been so long! How have you been?" Without pausing for a breath she continued, "I simply can't wait to tell you about my summer travels. Our first trip was to the ocean, and aren't otters the cutest little animals! I simply had to have an otter coat. When the wind is raw, I shall wear it to school and you may feel it."

Which one is she? Shannon wondered. She stole looks at the girl as her stories flowed on and on. Not only was she tall and slender, she was dressed in a style Shannon had seen only in *Godey's Lady's Book.* She even wore a watch pin fastened to her bodice. Her corset had to be breathtakingly tight to squeeze her waist so small, Shannon thought, and she wore a bustle, besides, to make it look even smaller. Shannon held her tummy in, and wished her papa would let her wear a corset, at least. "Bad for young bones and bodies," he had said.

The brown-haired girl was corseted, too, Shannon noticed. Her eyes met Shannon's and she smiled, but there wasn't a chance to speak. "We visited a geyser, as well," the first girl was saying. "I nearly swooned in surprise when it blasted forth and sprayed water all about! We all were drenched. And then there were the baths at the hot springs. The water smelled like rotten eggs! I couldn't bring myself to put even my littlest toe in." She paused to bring a lacy handkerchief to her nose.

"This is Jeanette," Betsy told Shannon quickly, pointing to the brown-haired girl. Jeanette smiled and nodded a silent *hello.*

"As I was saying," the tall girl began again, "we next visited the grandest canyon of them all. . . ." Shannon thought about how much all these trips must have cost. And the coat. And the dress. She shook her head. She'd never known anyone in all of Ireland with so much money to spend. It seemed impossible. Betsy didn't question any of it, so Shannon kept her doubts silent.

Rebecca rushed up to join them as they walked toward school. There were hugs and squeals and giggles all around, but none for Shannon. *These are the old friends Betsy was talking about,* she thought. Shannon felt big and clumsy and invisible all at the same time.

"Isn't it about time we all began our walking club again?" the tall girl was saying. "Remember all the fun we had last year, the four of us? The *Fabulous Four?*" Suddenly Shannon was listening closely. There wasn't any extra room inside of "Four." Her lunch pail handle slipped from her sweaty hand and clattered to the ground. The group of girls stopped while Shannon stooped to gather her lunch.

"And who have we here?" the fancy girl asked Betsy.

"Well, Margaret, it's high time you took notice," Betsy teased. Shannon stood up and tried to smooth her dress back into place. "This here is my new neighbor and friend, Shannon O'Brien."

"Oh, really?" Margaret said, her voice cool and empty. "And this is a friend of yours?" She flipped her watch pin up so she could read its face. "Oh dear, girls. I do think we are going to be late." She turned and hurried toward the school. The others followed behind her in a flutter of ribbons and ruffles.

What did I do wrong? Shannon wondered. *What did I say?* "You need to be strong in San Francisco," Mi Ling had told her. Shannon bit her lip and hurried along after Betsy's friends. ❖

CHAPTER TWO

MAKE YOUR MANNERS

"Why, she's pretty as a picture!" Betsy whispered.

"Who *is* she?" Margaret whispered from the desk beside Betsy's. "She looks simply dashing!"

Shannon just stared. Could this be their teacher? *Teachers aren't pretty,* she argued silently. *They are old and mean. Or they wear long black nuns' habits. Or both.* Shannon smiled. This woman was wearing a fancy lavender dress with a carved cameo pin at the neck. Her black hair was swept up into a mass of dainty ringlets. Shannon decided she had to be wearing makeup, too. No one could have such dark eyelashes or pretty cheeks unless they were painted on. "Miss Kennedy," it said in elegant script on the board. Shannon smiled at the familiar Irish name.

"Please rise." Miss Kennedy's voice was deep and rich and kind.

"How's *she* going to ride herd on the boys?" Betsy whispered as they got to their feet. Shannon looked down the long row of wooden desks. Margaret and Jeanette stood tall and still. Shannon tried to be as still. A boy held his hand to his heart and rolled his eyes as if he were in love with the teacher. The short boy next to him punched him in the arm. A third boy in a patched shirt stood at attention. Beyond the trio was an aisle and another six desks. She turned to look behind. There were more than a dozen rows of desks. *So many children!* she thought.

"Face front, please." Shannon turned quickly to meet the woman's bright blue eyes and gentle smile. "Kindly make your manners," the teacher said to the class. Beside her, Betsy and Margaret curtseyed, so Shannon did too. She sneaked a look down the row where all the boys were bowing.

"We will now sing 'America,'" the teacher said, turning to face an American flag hanging on the wall. She hummed a short, clear pitch for the song. Shannon stood, stunned. Betsy turned toward the flag, too, and Shannon copied her friend again. But when the entire class started to sing, "My county 'tis of thee . . . ," Shannon stood openmouthed. *I know that tune,* she thought. It was the same melody as "God Save the Queen." How the Irish hated that song!

Why would they sing that here? America had fought free of the British! Shannon listened for a moment, then had to smile. *They had changed the words. What a glorious joke to take an old British song and make it American!* Shannon's heart swelled with love for her new country. She pressed her hand to her heart to slow its racing beat.

While the class sang verse after verse of the song, Shannon remembered hearing Papa arguing back in Ireland. "Why do the Irish have to speak English?" he would say. "We had a perfectly fine language of our own." Or sometimes, "The Brits have bled us dry with taxes and given none of it back, even in the famine." *How Papa would love this song!* she thought.

"We will now pray," the teacher was saying. Chairs

scraped and rattled against the desks as everyone sat down and all heads were bowed. No one crossed him- or herself, so Shannon didn't either. That felt strange, wrong. After roll call, Miss Kennedy said, "Who will help me pass out copybooks?" Shannon raised her hand. "Will, George, and Shannon may help," the teacher said. Shannon jumped to her feet. She joined the lovesick boy and the patched one at the front of the room.

"That's not fair," Margaret hissed down the row of desks.

"You are new here?" the teacher asked quietly, handing Shannon a pile of blank books. The scent of rose water drifted from Miss Kennedy's clothes, from her hair, from her soft white hands.

"Just barely come, ma'am," Shannon said. The teacher smiled and nodded.

"Isn't she glorious?" Margaret sighed as Shannon gave her a book.

After she handed out the thirty-seven books, Shannon sat down at her desk and opened her copybook. "Using your best penmanship, class, write your name and the date on the first page of your book," the teacher instructed the students.

Shannon loved starting a new copybook. Anything might happen on its pages! A neat, round hole was cut into the desktop holding a little ink bottle. Shannon peeked into it. The inkwell was full. Beside it lay a goose feather. The feather's white vanes had been cut off for half its length, and the point was split in two and sharpened perfectly for writing. *This part of the year, at least, will be fine,* she thought. She picked up the feather quill and dipped it into

Welcome

the velvety black ink. Shannon checked to be sure that the ink had gone up into the hollow part of the quill and wasn't ready to drip onto the fresh, clean page. Satisfied, she wrote "Shannon Sarah O'Brien" and, below it, "September 1, 1880."

Beside her, Betsy sighed sharply. Shannon glanced at her friend's book. The letters of Betsy's name slanted crazily and sloped downhill. Her last name, Frye, ended with a big inkblot. Betsy was trying to soak up the blot with the corner of her handkerchief.

"Throughout this year you will enter your best writings into this book," the teacher was saying. "Take great care with it, for it will be on view for parents at the end of the term." Shannon blew proudly on her first page and watched the shiny swirls and curves of her name dry to a flat, rich black. "The first entry will simply be a sample of your penmanship, not of your composition. Please write the words to 'America' on the next page. Take your time."

Shannon froze. Margaret leaned forward, looked directly at her, and grinned a nasty grin. With a great flourish, she turned the page in her copybook and began writing. Shannon bit her lip and closed her eyes to stop the tears. She heard a quick rustle of skirts and smelled a whiff of rose water. When she opened her eyes, a printed paper lay on her desk. It was the music—and the words—to "America". Shannon smiled at Miss Kennedy, dipped her pen, and went to work.

"Excuse me, ma'am." It was Margaret. "I don't believe you have introduced yourself."

Shannon drew her breath. *Couldn't Margaret read the board?* "Oh, Land sakes!" The teacher laughed. "Forgive me, class. I am Miss Kennedy. Now, back to work before the ink dries and clogs your points."

Down the row, Margaret sat sharply upright. "*She* is Miss Kennedy?" she whispered angrily. "*I'm* being taught by someone named Kennedy?" Shannon watched as Betsy looked at Margaret, sighed deeply, and went back to work. Finally Shannon did, too.

After reciting sums and reading aloud from McGuffey's reader, Shannon felt restless. She ached to stretch her arms and move her feet. Her face felt stiff from concentrating. "You may have a twenty-minute recess," Miss Kennedy said, looking at the boys. "You probably haven't sat this still since school last year. I know it is hard." *How could she know?* Shannon wondered. *She is so kind!* "As long as you work this well," the new teacher promised, "there will be frequent breaks for you."

Outdoors, Shannon stood next to Betsy at the edge of a group of girls. "Isn't she the loveliest schoolmarm PS 43 has ever had?" someone asked.

"She's not such great shakes," Margaret said darkly, her voice loud enough to carry across the playground. Shannon looked around.

The boys played "crack the whip." The short boy anchored the game, swinging the others about. His feet barely moved. The boy in patched clothes ran desperately on the wildly whipping end of the line. *Will,* Shannon reminded herself, *and George.* She knew they liked the teacher. *Why didn't Margaret?*

"I've a new litter of puppies in the stable," Margaret said, "if any of you wish to see them on the way home today."

Shannon remembered the dear old dog she'd left behind in Ireland and felt her eyes fill with tears. "Puppies," she said. "Oh, I'd love to!"

"Well now," Margaret said to her over the other girls' heads. "I'm not quite sure there is room for each and *every* one of us. Perhaps you may visit another day." Shannon felt a silence thicken inside herself.

She stayed silent for the rest of the school day. When the school bell rang, everyone stood. "Kindly make your manners," Miss Kennedy told the class. She smiled at Shannon, but Shannon looked away. When the boys had bowed, and the girls curtseyed, Miss Kennedy continued. "I would like everyone to bring something dear to you to share tomorrow, something that will tell us more about yourselves. And do make your manners to your parents as you greet them today."

As the students filed out of the classroom, Shannon made the speech she'd been practicing since recess. "Dear Betsy," she said carefully. "You must go and see Margaret's puppies."

"Oh, not without you, pardner," Betsy said, as Shannon had known she would.

"I can't," she lied. "Papa expects me to work with him in the office after school."

"Well then." Shannon thought Betsy looked relieved as she said, "If that's the lay of the land, pardner, I will mosey over to Margaret's for a bit."

Shannon dodged away across the street between two carriages and headed for home, alone. ❖

CHAPTER THREE

A WILD IDEA

"Good afternoon, Papa." Shannon curtseyed, glad to find her father between patients when she arrived home.

"And what is it you're doin' there?" He looked at her in astonishment.

"The teacher told us to make our manners to our parents when we got home."

"I'm thinking I like this woman!" Papa said, laughing.

Shannon joined in the laughter for a moment, then grew silent. "Papa, not everyone likes Miss Kennedy." Shannon described how Margaret had seemed to love the new teacher. "Then, quick as a leprechaun's wink, Margaret went cold." She thought for a moment, picturing the walk to school that morning. "And she did the same with me."

"She was cruel to my wild rose?" Papa asked quickly.

"No, n-no." Shannon leaned against the examining table. "She's just not very friendly."

"There must be plenty of other lads and lassies there to befriend my bonny bairn. They'll soon learn what a fine person you are."

Shannon thought about the "Fabulous Four" in Margaret's walking club. "It isn't so simple as that," she said.

There was a knock at the door. Papa pulled his watch out of his vest pocket, held it out to the end of the watch chain, and popped open its carved gold lid. "Ah, and that will be Mrs. McNulty and her wee Tommy, on time as always. Care to stay and watch?"

Shannon caught her breath as Papa snapped the watch shut. *Stay and watch his doctoring?* She had never dared to do that. *What if Tommy starts bleeding?* she thought. *I could always just leave if it gets bad,* she promised herself. Shannon settled herself into a corner of the office as the door opened.

Mrs. McNulty didn't seem to mind at all that she was there. Tommy ran about the office, an empty sling dangling around his neck. "I see he's feeling better," Dr. O'Brien said with a chuckle.

"Oh, indeed." Mrs. McNulty cornered the child and stuffed his arm back into its sling. In a second it was out again, and he was using it to reach for a flask that was sitting on the shelf. Shannon grabbed the bottle before he could tip it over and spill the amber liquid inside. Mrs. McNulty smiled a silent *thank you* in her direction.

"From the looks of things, the bone is healed." Dr. O'Brien sat down on his great leather chair and managed to hold the squirming child in his lap. He felt Tommy's arm. "But I wouldn't be surprised if you need me again," he said. "A bairn this busy often finds trouble for himself."

Mrs. McNulty laughed and agreed. "There isn't a cabinet in the house he hasn't climbed, and him only three. I don't get much rest, that's for sure."

"Well, now you know what to look for with a broken bone."

"Aye," Mrs. McNulty said. "The child screams a fair bit, the bone is bent, it bruises up big and purple, and I bring him in to see you again."

"Sometimes you canna' see the bend in a broken bone," Dr. O'Brien said. "Only you be sure to hold it steady just as it is—leave the bend alone or leave it nice and straight—and bring him in to me."

"Thank you, sir," Mrs. McNulty said. "Will that be another fifty cents?"

"Yes. Give it to Shannon, will you? She'll put it in the till in my top drawer while I play with wee Tommy a bit."

Tommy's laughter filled the office as he looked at the watch fobs dangling from the doctor's watch chain. Shannon smiled, remembering how magical those silver charms had seemed when she was little. He had a shamrock, a St. Patrick's medal, and three fobs from his men's clubs in Ireland. Now there were two new ones from his Irish clubs here in San Francisco.

"Thank you," she said to Mrs. McNulty as Papa finally closed the door behind the woman and her son.

"Always play with a bairn if you have the chance," he said to Shannon as if he were teaching a new apprentice to help at the office. "That way when the child's in trouble, he knows you as a friend."

"Thank all the saints!" Another mother rushed through the door holding a screaming child in her arms. "His hand is bleeding bad and I could only hope you was in!"

Oh no! Shannon's mind went blank. There were red stains on the lady's dress and skirt, Shannon saw, and a towel was wrapped around the child's hand.

"Put him here," Dr. O'Brien said, clearing the leather examining table with a sweep of his arm. Papers and books flew to the floor.

"Oh, there's so much blood!" The mother was nearly sobbing. "He's bleeding to death!" Shannon stared at the blood and felt her stomach rise.

"No he's not." Dr. O'Brien's calm voice seemed to come from a great distance. "Get a bandage for me, Shannon," Papa said. Shannon couldn't move. *Don't look at it,* she told herself. But she couldn't stop staring. The room started to go dim and she felt faint.

"Shannon!" Dr. O'Brien said sharply. "Think about it later. I need your help *now.*" Suddenly Shannon's head cleared and she was reaching into the drawer of white cloths.

"That's my girl," Dr. O'Brien told her. "What happened, Mrs. Hennessey?" Papa pressed the bandage Shannon handed him against the cut.

"He was playing with his papa's razor," the mother explained. "He's ten years away from having a whisker, but he wanted to be just like . . . like . . ." Her voice caught. "I kept dabbing at the blood, hoping it would stop. Is he going to bleed to death?" Shannon felt her stomach rise again and tried to fight it down.

"This cut"—Dr. O'Brien gazed at the table—"isn't serious. It looks worse than it is."

Shannon couldn't believe how calm Papa sounded. "We'll just hold this tight until it slows down some," he went on. "Dabbing, or changing bandages, just keeps the blood flowing. Hand me another bandage, Shannon." He pressed it right on top of the first one. "This'll stop it for sure." He held the child's hand up over his head and took out his watch. Like Tommy, this little boy couldn't keep his eyes off the chainful of charms.

Shannon watched with admiration as her papa calmed the boy down. The mother was still sniffling. Shannon reached her fingers up her sleeve and pulled out her handkerchief so the woman could wipe her eyes. She picked the books and papers up off the floor and set them neatly on Papa's desk. "Another bandage, daughter," he said. She fetched it from the drawer and watched him peek under the wad of cloth covering the wound.

"Ah," he said. "The bleeding has stopped. Knife wounds are like that. They bleed a lot but close quick—*if* you hold them firmly." He looked again. "No stitches." He cleaned around the cut, then took the bandage Shannon held and wrapped the boy's hand several times with it. "Leave this on for two days," he told the mother. "Then wash the wound well, but gently. If it swells and gets red, feels hot, or pains him more, bring him right back."

"Oh, thank you!" Mrs. Hennessey cried. Shannon put the dollar fee into Papa's till, her head still feeling strangely light. As she left, the woman said, "You are certainly lucky to have an assistant like this one."

"Aye, that I am," Papa said, smiling at his daughter. Shannon stood straighter and tried to smile back. "That wasn't any too easy for you, was it?" he asked. She shook her head. "Stay with it and, strong as you are, it'll get easier." Shannon didn't think so, but she liked the praise.

"Will you show me how to tie up a bandage all tidy like that?" she asked.

"So then you'll be helping me again, even if there's bleeding?" Papa asked her. Shannon swallowed and nodded. "Well, ye canna' be here for the next patient. It's a delicate matter with her, and I'm not so sure she'd be easy with you hearing it all."

"That's fine, Papa," Shannon said, and hurried out the door.

"There you are, Shannon!" Mi Ling met her in the hallway. "Your mother is making visits to the neighbors, and I wondered where you'd gone off to. How was the school? Was it grand or small? Did you do sums and Bible verses and fancy penmanship exercises? Was there a spelling bee?" Her voice sounded lonely.

"The day was . . ." Shannon paused a long moment. "It was fine," she said firmly at last. "But I do have a problem you can help me with."

"Oh, anything!" Mi Ling said. "It was so very quiet here without you."

"Well," Shannon said, "I need to bring something with me tomorrow that tells a great deal about me. What shall I bring?"

"What about a picture from Ireland?" she suggested. "Or your calling card with the Irish shamrocks and the wild rose? Could you borrow a claddaugh?" Shannon pictured the old Irish symbol of two hands holding a crowned heart. The O'Briens had that sign of faith and loyalty on rings and picture frames. That *was* a possibility. How well Mi Ling knew her!

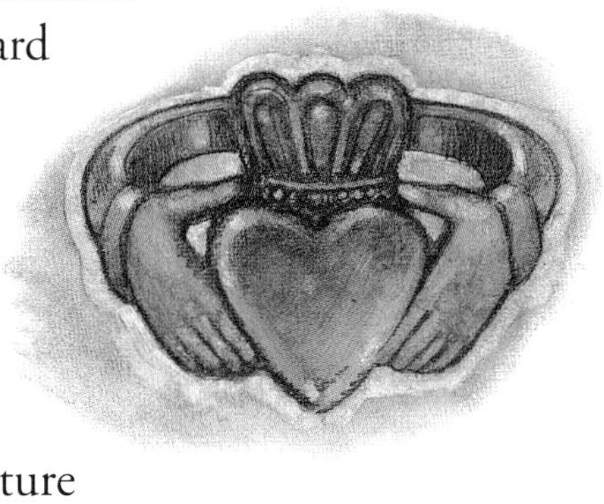

"What about the beautiful green wool shawl you wore on your way to America? Or your card from the brand-new library in town?"

"Oh, I just don't know!" Shannon told her friend. If it wasn't perfect, she didn't want to show it to lovely Miss Kennedy—or to Margaret. "It has to be something close to my heart," she said to Mi Ling. And then she knew the answer.

"Do you know the song 'America'?" she asked her friend. Mi Ling shook her head. "Let me teach it to you." They practiced it until supper time.

"Oh, Mamma," Shannon said at the dinner table. "You can't imagine what a lovely schoolmarm I have this year!"

Mrs. O'Brien helped Cook serve Papa and the children before she, too, settled down to eat. Then Papa talked about his day. He praised Shannon's helpfulness until she blushed. Mamma told about the neighbors she'd met and a club of Irish newcomers she had been invited to join at church. Shannon decided not to mention Margaret's club. Michael spilled his milk and cried until Nanny took him away, and finally, it was Shannon's turn to talk.

"Miss Kennedy is bonny and young and kind," she began.

"That doesn't sound like a proper schoolteacher," Mamma said. "Will ye be learning anything from her? Wouldn't it be better to be taught by the nuns?"

No! Shannon thought.

"Ah, Missus," Papa scolded her. "Mind that we're doing things the American way here. Give the lass a chance. We can always put our bairns into church school if this PS 43 doesn't work out."

Shannon smiled at Papa and went on. "We started our copybooks, did sums, and read aloud. I think Miss Kennedy was trying to find out what we already knew."

"And have you homework this very first day?" Mamma prompted.

"Indeed," Shannon said. "And it is the loveliest thing!"

"What?" Even Cook was listening in now.

"We must each bring in something that will show the class more about us," Shannon announced. She waited a moment. The O'Briens leaned forward. Shannon nibbled on her lip and swallowed hard. "I'm going to bring Mi Ling!"

"You'll do no such thing," Mamma said.

"But Shannon!" Mi Ling said. She sounded horrified.

Why isn't she happy? Shannon wondered. *She'll get to go to school after all.*

"Shannon, do ye know of what ye are doing?" Cook asked.

"No," Papa said to them. "I don't think she does." He looked at his daughter. "Think, Shannon. Ye must learn to think before ye act on a wild idea."

It isn't wild! Shannon thought. *It's right. Mi Ling* should *be going to school. Even Mamma said so.* She looked from face to face and took a deep breath. "Miss Kennedy said it would be fine."

There was a sudden silence around the table. "Shannon," Mamma said, her voice very serious. "Did she indeed say that?"

"Your good daughter would not lie to you now,

Missus," Papa defended Shannon, then turned to face her. "Would you now?" Shannon's eyes dropped to her lap. For the rest of the meal, she was quiet.

On their way out of the dining room, Papa stopped her. "Shannon," he said, "me wild, wild rose." She felt his hand resting on her red hair. "Will ye never be learning anything the easy way?" ❖

CHAPTER FOUR

A KINDNESS

"Top o' the mornin', Betsy," Shannon said, stepping out onto the O'Briens' porch as soon as her friend reached the top of the steps.

"Howdy!" Betsy said, turning to go to school.

Shannon didn't follow her friend down the steps. Instead, she said, "I can't wait to see what everyone brings to school today. What do you have?"

"You want to see it *now?*" Shannon glanced back toward her door and nodded. "Well," Betsy said, "I have it wrapped in my reticule here." She dug deeply into a drawstring purse as she climbed back up the porch stairs. "Here," she said at last. "It's a piece of lightning."

"What?" Shannon looked at the strange piece of rock. It was sandy on the outside, but a broken side glittered clear and shiny in the morning sun.

"When lightning strikes in the desert, it melts the sand grains into glass. You can dig it after it cools down." Betsy moved her hand, and sunlight lit the glassy green inside of the rock. "Cactus flowers bloom after a desert storm, but they last only a week. This lasts forever."

"Oh, may I hold it?" Shannon asked. Betsy handed it to her. It was cool and heavy and gritty. Where the glass was broken, it was sharp.

"We really have to skedaddle," Betsy said, "if we're ever going to get to school on time."

Mi Ling hurried out the door. She was wearing a new blue dress with a dropped waist and ruffled skirt. The blue ribbon in her hair matched the dress, but Shannon thought it looked wrong, somehow. *Her hair should have curls,* she realized. *Why didn't we think of that?*

"I suppose I'm ready, Shannon," she said.

Betsy stared at her in silence for a moment. "Land sakes, Shannon," she finally said. Her voice was flat.

"I thought it would be grand to bring Mi Ling to school," Shannon said quickly. "She has so many stories to share about her home in China, and her trip here, and being in the pet store. . . ." She broke off and waited for Betsy to say something.

"Well," Shannon tried to fill the silence, "everybody seemed to like Margaret's stories, so I thought . . ."

"Oh, Shannon." Betsy smiled sadly. She seemed about to say more. Instead, she shook her head, then turned and headed toward school.

"I did try to tell you," Mi Ling said to Shannon.

"Oh, and it'll all be fine," Shannon said, but she was beginning to have her doubts as she and Mi Ling hurried after Betsy.

They made their way silently through the traffic and up Bayview Street. A cluster of girls was waiting on the corner at the top of the hill. From the crowd's center, Margaret's hand popped up to wave. "Hurry, Betsy dear!" she called gaily. A few other girls called greetings, too, and smiled at them. *The Fabulous Four are there,* Shannon thought, *and lots of others.* She began to feel better about the day, the school, the year.

But as she and Mi Ling got closer, Margaret pulled her hand down and her gaze turned frosty. "Indeed, Betsy," she said as they joined the other girls. "Calling an *Irish* girl a *'friend'* is one thing, but this . . ."

All the chatter in the group died. The girls looked at Margaret. She spun silently and headed toward school. One by one, the others followed. Shannon and Mi Ling came last.

"Make your manners, please," Miss Kennedy asked, but no one was listening. "Class," she called. "Class, please come to attention." But they wouldn't.

"What's *she* doing here!?" a boy's voice came from the back. Another voice called, "Is that one of them blasted *Chinese?*" And, closer, a girl said, "She's crazy to bring that girl here!" Shannon sunk low in her seat. She could feel her cheeks burning.

"Jes' wait till my father hears about this!" Will snarled.

"Why, Will, isn't your dear papa on the school board?" Margaret asked, loud enough for all to hear. Will nodded.

"Shannon," Miss Kennedy said. "Kindly ask your friend to join us for a moment in the hallway."

Shannon led Mi Ling through the classroom. Rude whispers followed them until Miss Kennedy softly closed the door and turned to the girls. "I am sorry," the teacher said to Mi Ling, "but you must go home."

"But you said to bring along something I love," Shannon argued. "And Mi Ling is a dear friend who lives with me. She only wants to learn—"

"I did *not* ask you to break the law, Shannon," Miss Kennedy said. "What you've done disrupts my class and, further, it puts my job at risk."

"You are quite right, of course," Mi Ling said. "I have to apologize for Shannon. She has no idea how strong feelings run here in San Francisco." She sighed. "I tried to tell her, but . . ."

Miss Kennedy smiled at her. "Wait here a moment," she said, and with a quick rustle of rose-scented skirts, hurried back into the classroom.

"I'm sorry," Shannon said to her friend. It wasn't enough, but it was all she could say.

"There is no harm done to me," Mi Ling answered. "I've become used to it."

Shannon wanted to cry. They stood outside the classroom for what seemed like forever.

Finally, the teacher came out, carrying a sealed letter.

"Please hand this to Shannon's parents, um, 'Mi Ling,' is it?" The Chinese girl nodded. "Now, do you know the route home?"

"I can find my way, ma'am. It is Shannon who is a stranger in a strange land."

"Good," Miss Kennedy said, setting a slender hand on Mi Ling's shoulder. "And I shall speak with your loyal friend during recess."

No one would meet Shannon's eyes as she returned to her desk—not even Betsy. "Let us now sing 'America,'" Miss Kennedy said, and hummed a starting note for them all.

Shannon rose with the others and sang the words she and Mi Ling had practiced over and over. The morning passed in a blur of shame. When the others filed outside for recess, Shannon sat stiff in her seat.

"Shannon, dear," Miss Kennedy said, sitting down at the desk next to hers. "This surely was a hard morning for you."

Shannon felt tears threaten. *Don't cry,* she scolded herself. *Not in school.* "It's just not right!" She heard the quiver in her voice, and hated it.

"No, it isn't." Her teacher's calm voice helped. So did the scent of rose water. "Folks distrust things—and people—they don't understand. Many, many Chinese, and Irish, too, are moving into San Francisco. The old-timers don't understand the new folks' language and customs." Shannon nodded slowly.

"But there's more," Miss Kennedy went on. "The immigrants come here and get jobs."

Like Cook, Shannon thought, *and Nanny. And all the railroad workers Betsy's always talking about. And Papa, too.*

"People here are worried about losing their own jobs. They resent the newcomers."

"Does everyone in San Francisco feel this way?" asked Shannon.

"Some people are so full of prejudice that they can never think straight. Others can be won over by strength and patience and kindness. But it takes time."

Shannon sighed and sniffled. "Patient, I'm not," she said.

Miss Kennedy laughed, and after a moment, Shannon smiled. "Neither was I," the teacher said. "At least not at first. You have to practice patience. Now, I really must go and call the class in again. Are you all right?"

Shannon nodded. *She's Irish, too,* she thought. *She really does understand.* Margaret's sudden coldness after she heard the teacher's Irish name made sense now. And her cruel comments at the corner. *Margaret must be one of those people,* she realized—*full of prejudice.*

But was Betsy that way, too? Shannon's hands lay limp and cold on her desk.

She sat in her place through lunch, too, and never raised her hand to give an answer. When the last school bell rang, Shannon darted out of the classroom without speaking to anyone—not even Betsy. She had worried about it all afternoon. *Is Betsy prejudiced like all the others?* After everything else that had happened on this terrible day, Shannon didn't want to know. ❖

Chapter Five

Hot Water

"What is *wrong* with you?" Betsy stood at the doorway, morning sunlight glowing in her blonde hair. "You ran away from me yesterday after school. When I came to see you, your mother said you were busy. And now I've knocked and knocked on this dad-blamed door till my knuckles are plumb raw. . . ." She blew on the fingers of her right hand. "Why," she went on, "I reckon I'll only be able to do a half-good penmanship lesson today."

It was so good to see Betsy! Shannon smiled, picturing Betsy's sloppy handwriting. Half-good script was the best Betsy could do even when her hand wasn't sore. Shannon's smile spread. Then she began to laugh with relief and with the picture of what half of Betsy's half-good would look like.

"What's so all-fired funny?" Betsy demanded.

"You worrying on about your penmanship, as if you cared a fig."

Betsy said, "Oh." She paused and then said, "Now, Shannon, that's not fair. My writing is not *that* bad." Shannon fought to stop laughing and held herself quiet for a moment. "It may not be fair," her friend repeated, "but it *is* true, isn't it?"

The girls looked at each other and broke into laughter. They laughed helplessly until their breaths came in ragged hiccups. Shannon leaned against the corner post and smiled at Betsy. "You really *are* my friend, aren't you?"

"Did you doubt it?" Betsy said. She looked at Shannon a long moment. "Listen, girl," she said. "I'm like a cocklebur stuck in a horse's mane once I pick my friends. And you're one of them."

Shannon felt a warm rush. Betsy really *was* a friend. She thought of Betsy's other cocklebur friends: Jeanette, Rebecca, and Margaret. *Why did Betsy like Margaret?* she wondered.

Mrs. O'Brien leaned out the door. "And did you girls intend to be goin' to school this fine day?" she said.

"Land sakes!" Betsy jumped. "We'll be in hot water if we're late!"

The girls ran to the corner and hurried up Bayview Street. They waited for a coal wagon to pass before crossing the street and dashing to school. Together, they scampered up the steps, raced down the hall, turned into the classroom, and stopped.

Behind the desk where Miss Kennedy should have been stood a tall, brown-haired man.

Wrong room! Shannon thought and turned to flee. Betsy grabbed her hand and pulled her back in. There were Will and George. It *was* the right room—but where was Miss Kennedy? Betsy looked at Jeanette, who shrugged her shoulders. Margaret was simply facing front and glaring.

"Do we not know how to tell time, girls?" the teacher asked, stepping forward. "Do we not value education?"

"Depends on who's doin' the educatin'," Will muttered.

The teacher raised a switch. "I told you to mind your words, young man!"

Thwack! The switch slammed against the desk and broke in two, missing Will's hand by inches. The sound echoed in the total stillness of the classroom. No one seemed to be breathing.

"What do you have to say for yourself?" the teacher demanded.

"Sorry, sir."

"Louder!"

"I'M SORRY, MR. GAUL, SIR."

"Not sorry enough, I'll warrant." The teacher grabbed another fresh-cut switch from a pile on his desk. "But you will be if you speak out of line again this day." Mr. Gaul turned to write on the chalkboard. "Our school day commences when the bell rings, and I . . ." Here he left a blank space, and glared at the girls. He continued writing, "will never again presume to be tardy."

"Please fill in your name." He handed the chalk to Shannon. Yesterday she'd longed to try writing on this marvelous new invention. Today the blackboard looked so dark and evil she almost dropped the chalk. She stepped up to the board. Chalk dust filled her nose and choked her throat. Everyone was watching her, she knew, as she raised the chalk to start her name.

Kreeeee! The chalk screeched across the board. The hair on Shannon's neck stood up, but she didn't dare stop writing. *How did Miss Kennedy make it look so easy?* she thought. "Shannon Sarah O'Brien," she wrote, pressing harder.

"Thank you," Mr. Gaul said, his voice high and sharp. "Now, you." He thrust the chalk at Betsy.

Oh no! Shannon thought. *What would this awful man think of Betsy's penmanship?* But her friend grabbed the chalk, stepped up to the board, and wrote, "Elizabeth Anne Frye."

"That is dreadful," the teacher said. "Are you being deliberately unco-operative?" Betsy shook her head no. Shannon could see tears in her eyes. "Kindly erase that poor excuse for penman-ship," Mr. Gaul demand-ed, "and write your name properly."

Shannon prayed while Betsy wrote. At last she was done. It looked better, Shannon thought. A little better. The teacher stared at the board. "Handwriting is a mirror to character," he said to the class. "Penmanship this poor shows that the writer takes no pride in her work, and has no consideration of others who may wish to read her writing. You may be seated. You will remain at your seats through recess, copying this sentence one hundred times. Perhaps then you will learn the truth of it."

Betsy had no pride? No consideration? Shannon wanted to yell, to fight. Recess wasn't important, but Betsy was the best friend anyone could have. *Who* is *this man?* Shannon wondered as she walked to her desk. *Where is Miss Kennedy?* She would never have done this to anyone in her classroom.

The broken switch lay on Will's desk. Will sat as far away from it as he could get, as if it were alive and dangerous. *Will,* Shannon thought. His father was on the school board. And Miss Kennedy had said that having Mi Ling in class put her job at risk.

Shannon walked on down the row, thinking hard—and trying not to think at all. *Did Miss Kennedy lose her job? Because of me?* She sat down and tried not to cry. Betsy settled into the seat next to her.

All morning, whenever she looked up, she had to read "Our school day commences . . ." and look at her elegant signature above Betsy's awkward lettering. She knew that every other student in the room was looking at it, too.

"Oh, Betsy," she said when Mr. Gaul had left them at recess to write their sentences. "I'm sorry."

"The man's a sidewinder and a bully," Betsy said. To Shannon's surprise, she didn't sound hurt. Instead, she seemed angry. "Only no-accounts go after kids that way. I've seen men like that at the camps. I bet he's mean to his wife, too." She dipped her quill in the ink, bent over her paper, and began writing.

Shannon sat back and thought about Betsy. She was so strong to think that way. *But,* she thought, *she's right, too.*

And Shannon began to write, "Our school day . . ." She had just finished when the bell rang again. Mr. Gaul entered, carrying a switch. Thirty-five silent children marched in behind the teacher and settled into their seats.

"Open your books," he began. The *thwack!* of the switch sounded on a desktop whenever a student missed a sum or read a word aloud incorrectly. Shannon remembered seeing switches used on students who were rude to the teacher or who fought in the classroom. One of her teachers had pulled ears. Another nun had paddled the worst of the mean gang of boys in her class. That was only right. This wasn't. *And it's all my fault,* Shannon kept thinking. *It's my fault that Miss Kennedy lost her job.*

At the school's ending bell, Mr. Gaul said, "Attention." Everybody sat, silent. All day the classroom had been that way: silent, breathless, fearful. "I thank you for your cooperation," the man said. "I expect that, on the morrow, when Miss Kennedy returns, you will give her the same respect. You are now dismissed."

Miss Kennedy was coming back? Shannon jumped to her feet. She wanted to cheer, to hug Betsy, to clap her hands with happiness. But Mr. Gaul was glaring from the front of the room, switch in hand. Like everyone else, she walked out silently. *Mi Ling was lucky not to be here today,* she thought.

When she got out of the building, Shannon did cheer—like everybody else. "He was dreadful!" George said.

"I wanted to beat him up proper," someone else said. Many boys agreed with that. "I have a mind to ambush him on the street." "*He* should feel that switch!" Will didn't say anything at all.

"Well," Margaret said to the girls around her, "I, for

one, will be glad to see our dear Miss Kennedy's return." Shannon looked right at her. Just yesterday Margaret had seemed to dismiss the teacher because she was Irish, and now . . .

"Oh, indeed," Jeanette was saying. "Is the walking club ready to go? We could talk about all of this while we take our constitutional."

"Yes," Margaret announced. "If the Fabulous Four are ready . . ." She looked around at the group. A couple of girls wandered off. Then another one walked away. Finally there were five.

Shannon looked at her friend. Betsy was shifting from one foot to another. Shannon sighed. She wasn't feeling patient after this day. *What else had Miss Kennedy said to do?* she tried to remember. *Oh, yes: Be kind.*

Shannon took a breath and said, "I'm so sorry," loudly enough for all to hear. "I'd surely love to join you on your walk, but I have to work with my father this afternoon." *Maybe Mi Ling will be there to talk to,* she hoped.

Betsy squeezed Shannon's hand tightly, then left to join her other friends in the walking club. ❖

CHAPTER SIX

TWIN MYSTERIES

"If at first ye dunna' succeed, try, try again."

"Close, Shannon. Try saying 'yew' instead of 'yeh.'"

Shannon tried three times before she could copy the sound exactly. "Bully for you!" Betsy clapped. "Now, you must try to say 'don't' instead of 'dunna'.'" Over and over they practiced.

"I dunna' . . . no, I *don't* know how to thank you enough, Betsy."

"Land sakes, Shannon. I don't know why it's so all-fired important for you to sound like everybody else. I *like* the way you talk."

Shannon did not want to tell her friend how the boys teased her at recess whenever she recited in class. Or about how much she wanted to be part of the Fabulous Four on their daily walks. Or about the sign she'd seen in a store that had said NO DOGS. NO IRISH. NO BLACKS.

"It's for elocution class, Betsy. I want to get a perfect '1' on my monthly report for September." Shannon knew it wasn't the whole truth, but it wasn't a lie, either. "Besides, I like reciting speeches and poems. Best of all are the plays!" Shannon pictured herself in a class production, dressed as Juliet from Shakespeare's play perhaps, or Sarah from the Bible.

"You don't have to worry about your marks, Shannon. You're so good in grammar and mental arithmetic! How do you keep all the numbers straight in your head?"

"Miss Kennedy makes all of it seem easy, somehow," Shannon said.

"Except penmanship," Betsy added. They both laughed.

"So pull out your quill and we'll get to working on that," Shannon said. Betsy groaned, but she opened her ink bottle and began making rows of careful *O*s and *P*s and *S*s across a fresh sheet of paper. "Lovely," Shannon told her, and began her own practice lines. For a few moments, the only sound on the O'Brien porch was the scratching of quill points on paper.

"Miss Kennedy shared a new book with me," Shannon said, pausing to dip her pen into the ink. "It's called *Black Beauty*. It's all about a horse and his life and it's splendid. Would you like to borrow it next?"

"I'd a darn sight rather be *on* a horse than just reading about one." Betsy put her pen down. "It's Rebecca who loves to read. Remember talking about *Little Women* with her this summer? Couple of dang fools, you were, weeping over words on paper. You could tell her about this new *Black Beauty* book."

Shannon looked over the porch railing at the sunset. *Rebecca?* she thought, recalling how much she'd enjoyed discussing books with her in the summer. Shannon's eyes filled with tears just thinking about the story of the horse—and about the chance to share it with Rebecca.

"Did you ever find out where Miss Kennedy went that day?" Betsy asked.

"No. It's still a mystery."

"I love mysteries," Betsy said. "We talk about this one all the time on our walks. What kept her away that day? The doctor's office? A banking problem? A dress fitting? A sudden illness? A beau? Perhaps she's going to get engaged to a dashing young blade. That's what we all decided."

"Oh, I hope not," Shannon said quickly. "She's the best teacher I've ever had. I don't want her to have to quit. You know they'd fire her in a moment if she married. Or drank spirits. Or was seen in the wrong part of town. Teachers have to lead perfect lives nowadays to keep their jobs." She closed the ink bottle and took out her history book. "Besides, she looks far, far too young to be married."

"My sister, Alva, is only nineteen," Betsy began.

"Don't you be telling me she is marrying," Shannon said. "Mamma says women shouldn't marry until their late twenties—if then. They'll be sorry if they do. Everyone in my part of Limerick . . ."

A sudden silence beside her made her stop. "Betsy?"

"Top of the evening, Shannon. Howdy, Betsy." Mi Ling smiled as she climbed the porch stairs.

"Why, Mi Ling, where have you been keeping yourself?" Betsy asked quickly. "I haven't seen you in days!"

"No one has," Shannon said. "It's a big secret where she hides for hours and hours every day. Michael says she leaves every morning. And I can see she's gone every afternoon, too." Shannon looked at Mi Ling. "We never get to talk anymore."

"Oh, splendid!" Betsy said, grinning at Shannon. "Another mystery." She rubbed her chin. "Let's see if we can solve it. Mi Ling, are you going to the doctor's office?"

"No," Shannon said. "I would have seen her."

"Are you having banking problems? We millionaires do have such difficulty." Mi Ling shook her head no, and the girls all laughed.

"Are you going to have a dress fitted at the dressmaker's?" Betsy asked.

"Perhaps a crimson satin gown with ostrich plumes and bead fringe?" Shannon stood and paraded about, pretending to model a sinful bar girl's dress. The laughter was wild.

"Or," Betsy continued, "are you taken by a sudden illness . . . every single day?" Mi Ling pretended to faint onto the swinging porch settee, grasping at her chest and rolling her eyes.

"No, I'm fine," she gasped between giggles.

"Well, then, you must have a beau," Betsy pronounced. She pretended to twirl the end of a mustache and made a dramatic bow to the "dying" girl on the settee. Shannon waltzed over in her make-believe bar gown. She swatted the back of Betsy-the-beau's skirt, and the three girls collapsed in helpless laughter.

"We haven't solved Miss Kennedy's mystery," Shannon said later as they sat breathless on the settee. "Won't you give us a clue about *your* secret?" She looked at Mi Ling.

"Only that you would be genuinely pleased."

Shannon touched the good-luck shamrock hanging around her neck. "Do you suppose secrets come in threes," she thought aloud, "the way luck does?" She decided to watch closely for another mystery.

At the top of the hill the next morning, Shannon pulled *Black Beauty* from the pile of books she was carrying. She eased around behind Jeanette to reach Rebecca's side. Margaret glared at her, then kept talking, loudly, about an enormous party she was having. "Absolutely the most magnificent of the year." Shannon didn't listen. She knew she would not be invited.

"Rebecca," she said quietly. The girl turned quickly, looked at Shannon, and smiled. *I forgot how nice she is,* Shannon thought. "This is as good as *Little Women*—perhaps better. I think you'll like it. It's Miss Kennedy's, so I must have it back soon." She offered the volume to Rebecca and held her breath. The book trembled in her outstretched hand.

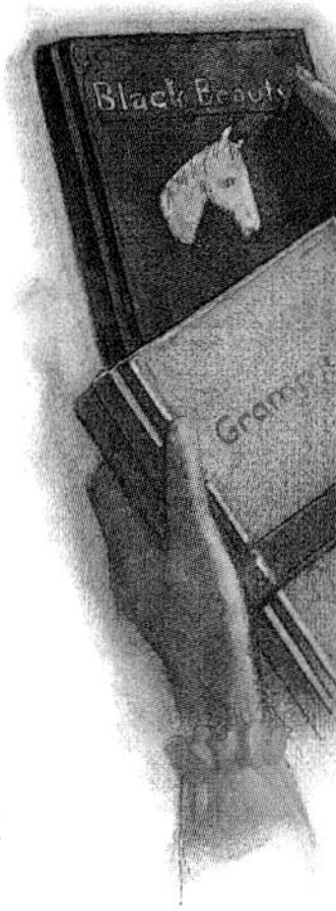

"Thank you," Rebecca said. She took the volume and tucked it into her book strap. "It would have to be deliciously fine indeed to merit that praise!"

"Land sakes," Betsy said from behind her. "Doesn't Rebecca talk just like a book!"

Rebecca blushed and looked down. "I love to hear her talk," Shannon said. Rebecca smiled.

"Oh, ladies," Margaret called. "We'd best be hurrying on to school, don't you think?" She looked directly at Shannon, then led the group back along Bayview Street.

After school, Shannon excused herself as she did every day now, saying, "Papa's waiting." *At first it was a fib,* she thought. *But now he really does expect me.* All the way home she thought of the things he'd shown her. How to knot the threads used for stitching wounds. She'd watched him take out tonsils, first calming the patient with laughing gas. How her stomach had clenched at that! But only at first. She'd seen infections and rashes and colicky babies, knife wounds and burns and unsteady old ladies.

She no longer bothered to look for Mi Ling. She knew her Chinese friend would be off somewhere on her mystery, and home by dinnertime. Then Betsy would arrive after dinner for a long hour of laughter and friendship and homework. It seemed to Shannon that September was flying by. *If the Fabulous Four would just be friendly to me,* Shannon thought, *everything would be perfect.* But Miss Kennedy had said to be patient, and patience took practice. ❖

Chapter Seven

The Third Mystery

A week later, there was a knock on the office door. Shannon opened it and saw Rebecca with Miss Kennedy's *Black Beauty* in her hand.

"Dear Shannon, this was indeed a most excellent book." Rebecca peeked in to look at Dr. O'Brien. "Excuse me for interrupting you in your office, sir, but the maid invited me in."

"No, no, no," Shannon's father said quickly. "It's a fine day when this papa sees another bonny young face smiling beside his own bairn's." He glanced at his pocket watch, then added, "It's far too rare a sight."

Hush, Papa! Shannon wanted to say, but she knew there was no stopping him once he got going. "Why don't ye take a wee bit of time for a cup of tea with this new friend, Shannon. I'm sure Cook would be havin' somethin' sweet a-baking."

Was that all he was going to say? Shannon smiled her thanks to Papa and led Rebecca into the hall. "Did you finish the book so soon?" she asked. "It's been only a few days!"

"Once I commenced reading, I simply couldn't stop," Rebecca said. "How dreadful to think that horses suffer so."

Shannon shook her head. "I don't pass a wagon on the street without thinking of Beauty." She was careful to say "don't" the way Betsy had taught her.

"I see Ginger everywhere," Rebecca agreed. "Poor, poor thing."

"I had never considered horses' feelings before," Shannon said. "I've taken to riding on the weekends with my papa." The words tumbled out. "There is a big black at the stable who is just as sweet as Beauty was. I think I could love him as dearly as the mistress did in the book. Betsy says I am a 'durn fool' to think of a horse as a friend. But when I shut the door to his stall he seems so lonely. . . ."

There was a strange silence. "I feel as you do," Rebecca said finally. "Has Miss Kennedy suggested any other titles to read?"

"No, and I've not been reading so much this week. I'm wanting my marks to be perfect, and the tests are only days away."

"Surely *you* don't have to worry about marks," Rebecca said.

Shall I tell her about that new college in Philadelphia? Shannon wondered. *The one just for women who want to be doctors?* But Rebecca kept on. "You've done so much for Betsy," she said. "We're all overjoyed with the improvement in her penmanship."

They've been talking about me, Shannon thought. "We have such fun sharing our skills," she said. "Betsy is teaching me, too, you know."

"I can't imagine what *you* would need to learn. I do wish someone could teach Jeanette," Rebecca said, sighing.

"She's in dire trouble with her arithmetic, and I worry that her father will thrash her soundly for the marks she is earning."

"Oh, no!" Shannon said. "Poor Jeanette."

"Alas, it may be so. But I must go now and meet the girls. Shall we speak again after the tests? Perhaps I can meet your friend, the horse." Shannon glanced at Rebecca, but the girl was grinning. "And we can read aloud together."

"To the horse?" Shannon teased. They both laughed. "It would be heaven," Shannon said, and walked Rebecca to the door. *Heaven.*

That evening, as Betsy climbed the porch steps, something slipped from her hand and clattered down the steps. "What's that?" Shannon asked. She leaned over quickly to pick it up.

"My button string," Betsy said. "And thanks for reaching it for me." She sighed and pulled at her corset. "Sometimes I wish I didn't have to wear this stiff old thing."

"What's this for?" Shannon held the long ribbon in her hand. Buttons of different colors and sizes had been sewn to it for half its length.

"Well," Betsy began slowly. "We make those to use for mending clothes after we are married."

"Why, Betsy," Shannon teased. "Don't tell me you're getting married!"

"Oh, Shannon, I know how you feel, and it makes it so all-fired hard for me to talk to you."

"Betsy, you *aren't* getting married!" Shannon was horrified.

"Land sakes," Betsy laughed. "Not *me.* But Alva *is* and I'm so excited and I couldn't tell you because I knew how you felt and . . ." Betsy took a quick breath. "I really want your help to get things ready and I hope you won't be upset."

Now it was Shannon's turn to take a breath. "I'm not a very good friend if you can't tell me secrets." *Prejudiced,* Shannon scolded herself. *That's what I've been. Thinking my Irish ways are the only right ways.* She swallowed hard. "I'm sorry, Betsy. I'm really happy for Alva. What can I do to help?"

"Thank you," Betsy said. "You can help if you have any old buttons." Betsy held out the long string. "Each one of these is from a good friend or a favorite old dress. Of course, some have to come from a papa's shirt or union suit." Betsy blushed at the mention of a man's long underwear.

"You don't have to pull them right off Papa yourself, do you?" Shannon teased.

"Oh, no!" Betsy said, then laughed. "Well, do you think you can help me?"

"Let's go look in Mamma's button box right now," Shannon said.

"She brought these all the way from Ireland?" Betsy ran her fingers through hundreds of different-colored buttons. There were big coat buttons and smaller ones from shoes or the wrists of kid gloves. There were studs from men's cuffs and shirt buttons, shoe buttons, hooks and eyes, and tiny little buttons from the necks of nightgowns and christening gowns. "Are you sure we may take a few?"

"Take more than that," Mrs. O'Brien's voice said from behind them. The girls turned and Shannon held up Betsy's button string to show her mother. Betsy explained what it was for.

"Give her my congratulations," Mamma said. Shannon knew Mamma had Irish ideas about marriage, too, but they didn't show in her voice. "Shannon," Mamma went on, "take enough so you can start a button string of your own to give Alva."

"Thank you, Mamma." Shannon looked closely at the chain draped across her lap. "Betsy, where do you get such a string?" she asked.

"It's a lace from a corset. I'll bring one to school tomorrow," Betsy promised.

"You could unlace yourself right now, as much as we care!" Mamma teased. Betsy looked horrified. She shook her head and blushed bright pink. Shannon and Mamma just laughed.

"Before you go," Shannon asked as they closed their books for the night, "I have a favor to ask of you."

"I would do anything for a friend as good as you, pardner," Betsy said.

Except stand up for me to Margaret, Shannon thought in a quick rush of anger. *Why doesn't she?* Shannon wondered, and suddenly sat up straight. *There's the third mystery!*

"Well?" Betsy was wiping her pen point clean with a soft cloth. Shannon didn't know how to ask about Margaret. *Patience,* she told herself.

"Would you mind if I invite Jeanette to study with us a few nights?" Shannon asked instead. "Just until the tests? Would that be agreeable to you?"

"Sakes alive!" Betsy answered. "Do you really have to ask? Let's us see if she can join us tomorrow."

Betsy stepped off the porch, waited for a buggy to pass in the fog, and crossed the street to her house. By the street lamp, she turned and waved. Shannon stood, practicing patience, long after Betsy had gone in and closed her door. ❖

CHAPTER EIGHT

COCKLEBUR FRIENDS

"Oh, blessed be!" Jeanette cried as she read her monthly report. "Papa will be so pleased!" Her eyes met Shannon's, and she nodded and said a silent *thank you.* Around them, their classmates were tearing open their envelopes.

"You look at your report cards before your parents see them?" Shannon asked the students standing on the school steps. They were all too busy to answer. Some gasped as they read their monthlies. Others sighed. Will pushed his way through the group, his face crimson with anger. Shannon watched George tuck his monthly report into his shirt pocket, then gently pat it. He was smiling broadly.

At last Shannon let herself peek into her envelope. It felt strange to be the first in her family to see it. Reading her marks, she had to smile. Except for one subject, she had all 1s! "Betsy, dear," she told her friend. "With your help, I got a 2 on my elocution! I *dunna'* know how to thank *ye* enough!" Shannon winked and the two friends laughed.

"Oh, but Shannon!" Betsy said. "*Look* at what you've done for my penmanship! I also got a 2! She held up two proud fingers for everyone to see. "This caps the climax!

I've never done better than a 4 in my life! My mamma will swoon."

"My folks said they'd buy me a pony if I did this well," Jeanette said. "I hope they meant it." *Any pony of Jeanette's would be happy,* Shannon thought. *It wouldn't be another Ginger.*

"I don't give a hoot about all your mamas and papas," Margaret said suddenly. "And you needn't make such a frolic of this here in the street. It's time we went home."

"Oh, Margaret." "Oh, I'm so sorry." "Oh, poor, dear Margaret." The girls around Shannon were suddenly cooing. "Oh, Margaret . . ." *Why?* Shannon wondered with a flash of anger. *It isn't just Betsy. Everyone is nice to Margaret, no matter how rude she is!* The girls were all rushing after her to the corner—and Shannon found herself hurrying along, too.

"Just go home, all of you," Shannon heard Margaret say as she fled ahead of them into the street.

Suddenly, motion seemed to slow down. "Git back!" a rider screamed as his horse bolted down the street. "Whoa!" a driver yelled as his horses reared with surprise. The wagon veered sideways as the driver fought to control his team.

Shannon saw it all—but she couldn't stop any of it. The side of the wagon swung toward Margaret. A crate fell off and smashed into the street. Hundreds of little glass medicine bottles shattered and clattered and slithered about on the cobblestones. Margaret slid and went down to her knees. Jeanette ran to help her, but tripped on a broken bottle and fell against the curbstone.

Rebecca started screaming. "Oh no! Oh, Margaret!"

Not blood! Shannon thought furiously. *Don't let there be a lot of blood!*

But there was. Margaret sat on the street, holding her knee, rocking and sobbing. Blood flowed down her leg and over her shoe buttons. Rebecca was still screaming. Shannon looked around. Somebody had to do something! She looked at the horses. The wagon driver had his team under control, though barely. She stared at the blood and her stomach began to do flip-flops.

"Think about it later," Papa's calm words came to her. "She needs your help *now!*" Shannon knelt beside Margaret and said, "How bad is it?"

"I can't bear it!" Margaret sobbed. Shannon gently lifted her skirt to see a deep cut above her high-topped shoe.

"Land sakes," Rebecca gasped. "Wipe off the blood!" She covered her face and began screaming again.

Rebecca is just making things worse, Shannon thought as she pulled a handkerchief from her sleeve. She pressed it right on the wound. "It's not bleeding that badly," she told Margaret in a calm voice. "Rebecca," she said loudly, "go find a policeman or get Margaret's mother." Rebecca stared at her blankly. "Go *now.*" Rebecca nodded, and hurried up the road.

"Doesn't Shannon *know?*" Jeanette asked Betsy, her voice angry. She sat next to Margaret, holding her own elbow. Tears were streaming down her face. Shannon looked at Jeanette's arm. No swelling, and no color yet. *It's probably not broken,* she thought.

"Give me another handkerchief," Shannon said to no one in particular. She held her hand up into the air and felt someone press a larger cloth against her palm.

"What else can I do?" It was a man's voice.

"Do you have a horse?" Shannon turned to ask.

The man nodded. "And a wagon." He waved at a low farm wagon waiting in the street. "I just delivered my load of flour, so I've room to carry anyone to the hospital as needs to go."

"When I get the bleeding stopped, I need someone strong to carry Margaret to my father's office, three blocks from here."

"Your father really *is* a doctor?" Margaret sniffled. Shannon nodded and tied the larger handkerchief tightly around the wound. "That's why you are so calm," Margaret added.

"Oh, no," Shannon said. "I'm not calm at all. I think I'm going to be sick—but it will have to wait until later. Now, put your hand just here."

Margaret stopped crying and helped press on the wound. "You are indeed calm," she said, "and really kind. Thank you."

"Shannon, what should I do about Jeanette?" Betsy asked.

"I don't think her bone is broken," Shannon said, "but my papa should still take a look at it." She stood as the man picked Margaret up in his arms. "Keep her leg high," she cautioned, "or it may start bleeding again." He settled her into the wagon, and Betsy and Shannon helped Jeanette climb in. Rebecca came panting down the sidewalk, followed by a policeman.

"Looks like everything is under control," the officer said.

"It is, thanks to this little lady here," the farmer said, pointing at Shannon. He helped Rebecca into the wagon and drove on down the hill toward the O'Briens'.

The girls waited in the hall outside Dr. O'Brien's office.

"Do you think she'll be all right?" Jeanette asked. Shannon noticed the girl rubbing her arm.

"Yes," Shannon said. She thought a moment, then decided to ask. "Why were you so upset with me on the street?" She looked from Betsy to Jeanette to Rebecca. "What is it I don't know about Margaret?"

The girls looked at one another. Finally Rebecca nodded.

Just then Cook brought out a tray. "Oh, and won't your mamma be proud when she gets home!" She winked at Shannon. "Girls, come have a wee bite of sweets in the parlor until the mister is finished doctoring."

The girls followed the scent of chocolate. "Delicious!" Rebecca said as she bit into a warm chocolate cookie.

"Thank you so much," Betsy said, sipping a fresh, cold glass of milk.

"Betsy," Shannon said as Cook carried their empty glasses away toward the kitchen. "Please tell me."

"Shannon, Margaret's mother died last year," Betsy said.

"And her papa ran away from the sorrow," Jeanette added.

No wonder Margaret was so prickly and stiff! "Is she all alone?" Shannon asked.

"No. No. She has us," the girls said quickly. Shannon looked around at the circle of worried faces. *They've all been protecting their friend!*

"She lives with her uncle."

"Poor thing!" Tears stung the corners of Shannon's eyes. "Is there anything I can do to help?"

"Just be patient with her," Jeanette said.

Shannon looked at Betsy. "I'll be a cocklebur friend to her. To all of you."

"Shannon!" It was Papa's voice. "Bring everyone in here, please."

"Now, that was some fine doctoring, Shannon my dear," Papa said when they had all filed into his office. "I'd have known the knots on that bandage anywhere." Margaret was lying on the examining table, her foot bare and her knee freshly bandaged.

"Did you get that good and clean before you bandaged it?" Shannon asked him.

"And who are we callin' the doctor here?" Dr. O'Brien pretended to look around his office.

"Oh, Papa," Shannon said with a laugh, "you, of course."

Dr. O'Brien gave a huge, patient-sounding sigh and answered, meekly, "Yes, dear. It's stitched—and very, very clean." He winked, and suddenly everyone was laughing.

"Shannon," Margaret said from the table. "Your papa says I'm not going to be walking much soon. After the way I've treated you, you didn't have to be so kind to me there in the street." She paused. "You could be part of the Fabulous Five, if you wish." *The Fabulous Five? They've made room for me!* Shannon blinked against quick, happy tears.

"At last!" Rebecca cried. From her seat deep in the leather chair, Jeanette grinned.

"Margaret," Betsy asked, "we could all visit with you and your puppies while your knee is healing, can't we?" Shannon smiled and looked around at her new circle of friends. ❖

CHAPTER NINE

SOUR PICKLES

"There's Mi Ling!" Betsy shouted as they got Margaret settled on the couch in the parlor. "Mi Ling, come and see our surprise guests!"

Mi Ling came into the room from the front hall and shyly said hello to everyone.

"Who brought you home?" Betsy asked. Mi Ling just smiled and shook her head.

"I can answer that," Jeanette said from the window. "Miss Kennedy. Look, she's just leaving."

Shannon ran out of the room and onto the porch. "Wait!" she called to the teacher. Miss Kennedy looked as if she wanted to hurry away. "Please wait," Shannon called. The teacher hitched her carriage and joined Mi Ling on the porch stairs.

"Do you know what's been keeping Mi Ling so busy?" Shannon asked as they entered the house. Miss Kennedy slowly pulled off her gloves. "If you do, please tell me. Mi Ling won't give me a clue, and I'm beginning to worry about her."

Miss Kennedy laughed and said, "Show her, Mi Ling." The Chinese girl reached into her reticule and pulled out a copy of a monthly report card. Shannon looked at the top line. "Mi Ling," it read.

"But . . . ," Shannon said. "I thought school was one of those things ye canna' change. . . ."

"You and Mi Ling argued so well that she should go to school that the very next day I took her over to visit a friend of mine who teaches at the orphanage. Mi Ling helps with the little ones there all day long, and in the afternoons I work with her in secret. She has such talent. . . ."

The teacher smiled warmly as her Chinese student wandered out into the hall along with Betsy.

The teacher turned to Mi Ling. "May your friends read your marks?" Mi Ling grinned and nodded.

Shannon opened the report card. A row of perfect 1s led down the side of the paper.

"My Land!" Betsy said. "If that isn't the prettiest report I ever saw!"

"But, girls," Miss Kennedy said. "You mustn't tell anyone that I'm teaching her. You do understand . . . I could lose my job."

"We'll never tell," Shannon promised. "But Mamma and Papa know, right?" Miss Kennedy nodded. "I think there's one other person who should know about this." She led them back into the parlor.

"Mi Ling??" Margaret repeated. "But she is Chinese! They can't learn . . ."

Shannon handed her the monthly report and smiled as Margaret read the marks. *The Fabulous Five,* Shannon thought, *sounded so bonny. But the Spectacular Six would be even better!*

"Margaret," Shannon asked, "do you think Mi Ling

could come and see the puppies sometime?" Margaret looked like she'd bitten a sour pickle. Shannon wanted to laugh.

"Perhaps next week?" Margaret finally managed to say.

"Bully for you!" Betsy whispered in Shannon's ear.

Margaret was still shaking her head in disbelief. *This wouldn't be easy,* Shannon thought. *Patience,* she reminded herself. *Strength and patience and kindness . . .* ❖

AFTERWORD

JOURNEY TO 1880

Imagine starting a school day without rising to say the Pledge of Allegiance. No one ever pledged "allegiance to the flag . . . and to the Republic for which it stands" in 1880. Those familiar words weren't written yet! Instead, before daily lessons began, classes sang "America" together, recited poetry, stood and did warm-up exercises at their desks, prayed and read Bible verses aloud, or listened to their teacher's lectures on behavior and manners. A school-marm or -master was hired to make the students learn their lessons. Learning, they thought back then, could be done only in a strict and serious setting. Learning came first, and respect and obedience were almost as important; whether you liked the school or the teacher didn't matter. Nobody cared about making the class interesting or fun, either. School wasn't entertainment; it was education.

The Denman Grammar School in San Francisco, c. 1880.

Teachers were free to hit anyone who got in the way of learning. If, in the 1880s, you were daydreaming or fell asleep at your desk, you might get your ears "boxed." The impatient teacher would slap the side of your head with his or her hand cupped. Your ears would ring for hours, or days, after a good boxing. Sometimes hearing was impaired for a lifetime. Nobody dozed off twice!

But teachers didn't just use their hands. Switches were displayed in many classrooms. If you misbehaved, you could expect to feel the stinging pain from a whipping with these long, thin branches. Your teacher might also use a paddle to spank you or a ruler to rap your knuckles. The pain was supposed to teach you a lesson about interrupting others' chance to learn.

Teachers had other ways of making you think about your errors, as well. Being told to write a sentence one hundred times was a common punishment. Try it someday, to see how very long it takes! If you were loud or disruptive, you might spend a half hour huddled under the teacher's desk, or a half day locked in the darkness of a closet while you "learned your lesson."

Sometimes teachers used peer pressure—and embarrassment—to force children to do their best. A lazy student might have to sit facing the front of the class wearing a "dunce cap" or a sign around his neck that said SLUGGARD.

Bad teachers had to do all of these things to keep control in their classrooms. Good teachers knew that kindness, interesting lessons, challenging goals, and warm praise worked, too. Most of them had to learn this on their own. There were a few "normal schools" that taught high school graduates how to teach, but many teenagers simply took a

Children playing "Drop the Handkerchief" on the last day of school in the early 1890's.

test of their knowledge when they finished school. If they passed the test, they were allowed to teach—and to control their classes however they could.

Students were expected to master reading, composition, elegant penmanship, arithmetic, civics, government, elocution, and history. If there was time, and the teacher was interested, nature study, art, and music might be taught, but only after the basic lessons were learned. By law, all children had to go to school in 1880 in San Francisco. All children, that is, except Native Americans—and the Chinese.

One-fifth of all people in San Francisco in 1880 were Chinese. None of them was allowed to become a U.S. citizen or to vote, so the Chinese could not change the many laws that were passed against them. It was against the law for them to go to public school or to be admitted to the San Francisco Public Hospital. They weren't even allowed to use their traditional wooden poles to carry packages in the streets! The Chinese made their own schools for their children. They had their own unofficial government, too, that helped newcomers move into Chinese society.

Another fifth of San Franciscans were Irish. They arrived already knowing how to speak English, and they could, after a few years, become U.S. citizens and vote. That made it easier for them to learn the political system and to use it to get ahead. Irish children, like all others (except Chinese and Native Americans), had to go to school. The Irish used their free education to move up from poverty to power.

The Chinese had to wait far longer to overcome the prejudices against them in San Francisco than the Irish did. Today both of these old immigrant groups are fully Americans, voting for laws that protect everyone, from Native Americans to the newest immigrants. How did they do it? They stayed strong and never gave up trying. They were kind, helping other newcomers with housing, jobs, and information about this new country. And they were patient, working long and hard for the changes that have finally come. ❖

A class portrait from the Silver Street Primary School in San Francisco, 1885.